W9-BWZ-326

Memorial Day Surprise

Memorial Day Surprise

by Theresa Martin Golding

Illustrated by Alexandra Artigas

Boyds Mills Press

To Mary C. Golding and in memory of Joseph M. Golding, and for all those who have served their country well.

—T. M. G.

To Nicolas and Andrei,
my source of happiness and inspiration

—A. A.

Published by Boyds Mills Press
A Highlights Company
815 Church Street
Honesdale, Pennsylvania 18431
Printed in China

Publisher Cataloging-in-Publication Data (U.S.)

Golding, Theresa Martin.
Memorial Day surprise / by Theresa Martin Golding ; illustrated by Alexandra Artigas. — 1st ed.
[32] p. : col. ill. ; cm.
Summary: When Marco attends a Memorial Day parade, he is surprised to see a familiar face among the veterans.
ISBN 1-59078-048-5
1. Grandfathers — Fiction. 2. Memorial Day — Fiction. 3. Veterans — Fiction. I. Artigas, Alexandra, ill. II. Title
[E] 21 PZ7.G653Me 2004
2003108158

10 9 8 7 6 5 4 3

"Is it a really big surprise, Mama?" asked Marco.

"Oh, yes," said Mama. "It is a very big surprise.

"But we must hurry. The parade will start soon."

Marco held Mama's hand tightly and walked faster. Many people were leaving the porches of their brick-row houses. Children skipped down the steps of the big apartment building. Abuelo, Marco's grandfather, lived there on the fifth floor, but Mama said there was no time to stop. What could the surprise be that made Mama rush so? They always stopped to visit Abuelo.

Marco watched the flags dance in the breeze. "What is memory day, Mama?" he asked.

Mama smiled. "It is called Memorial Day," she said. "But memory day is a good name, too. It is a time to remember some special people."

"Who, Mama?"

"You will see," she said.

"Beep! Beep!" Two girls swooped past Marco. Red and blue streamers fluttered from their bicycles and swished in the wind. Everyone was in a hurry to get to the parade.

FOR
SALE

When they reached the avenue, Marco's eyes opened wide. All the stores where Mama liked to shop were closed. The sidewalks were crowded with people sitting on folding chairs or colorful blankets. Two boys were even sitting on top of the big, blue mailbox!

Marco heard someone calling his name. "Look, Mama!" He pointed across the wide avenue. "Jenna is here, too! Is this the surprise?"

"No, Marco," Mama answered. "The surprise is even more special than seeing your best friend at the parade."

Marco sat on the curb with Jenna. The sun was hot on the top of his head. The big avenue seemed different without its zooming cars and rumbling trucks. It was like a rushing river that had run out of water.

Marco jumped up. "Did you hear that?" he asked. The faint *brrump bump bump* of a drum sounded in the distance.

Marco held his breath as the band marched closer and stopped right in front of him! The leader slowly raised his baton and the music burst into the air—horns and drums and the clash of the cymbals. Marco stood very still. The music was inside him, alive and jumping in his chest. *Boom! Boom!* He felt a thunder in his stomach. *Crash! Crash!* It tingled down his arms. Batons flew in the air. Pom-poms swooshed. Feet stamped in rhythm and the band moved on.

Marco wished Abuelo could have heard the music. Maybe it would have made his legs tingle again. "Was that the surprise, Mama?" Marco shouted. "Was it? Was it?"

"No, Marco," Mama said. "The surprise is even more special than the marching band."

A siren screamed and Marco jumped. A long red fire engine rolled down the avenue, its lights spinning and flashing. A firefighter walked beside the big engine. He stopped and shook Marco's hand. He gave Marco a little flag.

Marco waved the flag at the noisy fire truck. "Was that the surprise, Mama?"

Mama shook her head. "No, Marco. The surprise is even more special than meeting a real firefighter."

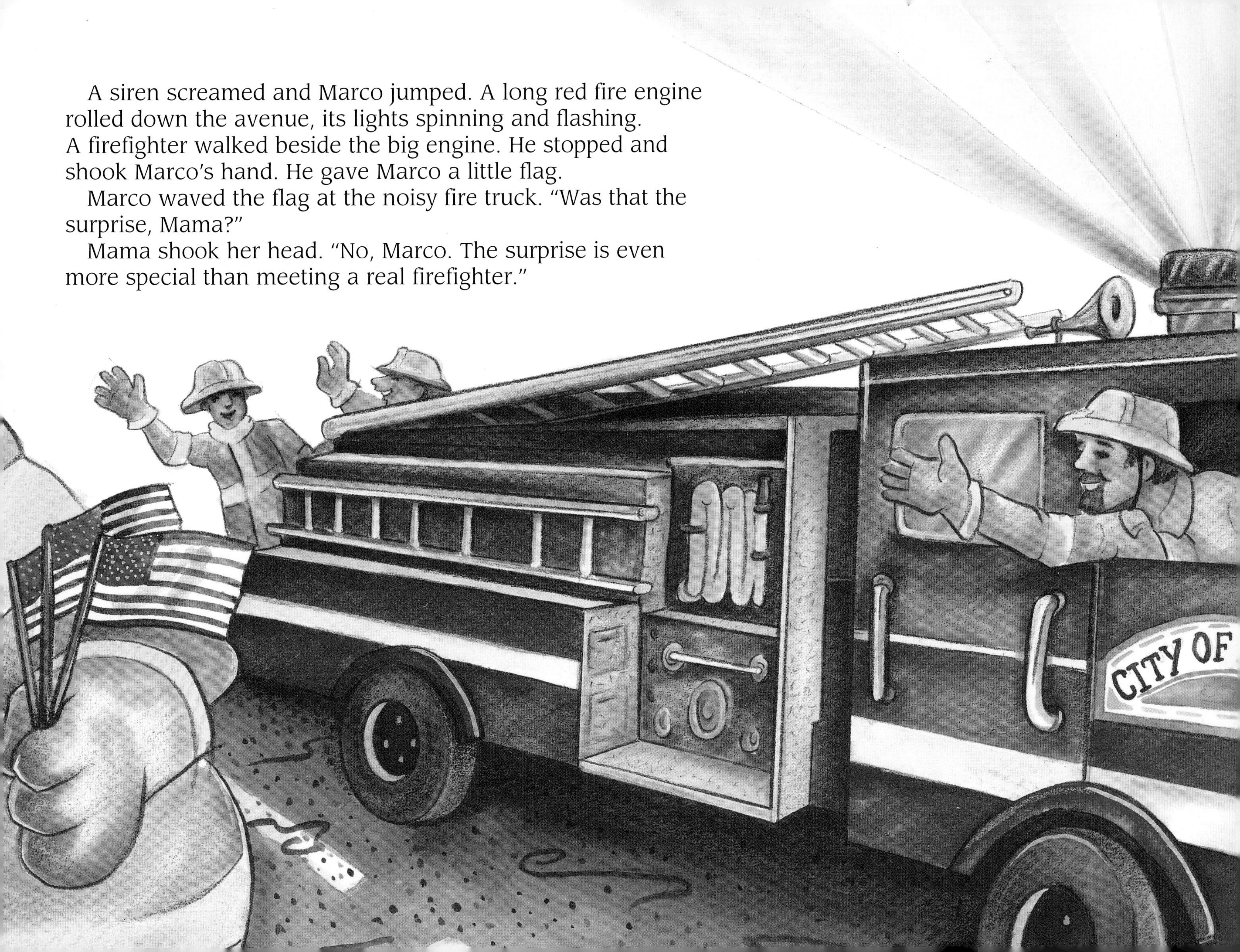

IN GOD WE TRUST

"Look!" Jenna shouted.

A truck was pulling a big float right down the street. It was the Statue of Liberty! A man with a dark beard stood in front of the statue. With his tall hat and long face he looked just like Abraham Lincoln.

Jenna frowned. "They are throwing things at people," she said. "That is not nice."

"It's candy!" screamed Marco.

Marco and Jenna dropped to the ground and scooped up all the candy that fell at their feet.

"Mama, look!" Marco opened his fist and showed her all the sweets he had collected. "That was the surprise, wasn't it?"

"No, Marco," Mama said. "The surprise is even more special than catching candy at the parade."

Marco put a butterscotch into his pocket. He would give it to Abuelo when he told him all about this parade.

What was happening? All the people stood up and began clapping. Marco could not see. There were no sirens, no band, and no falling candy. Still, the clapping became louder.

Men and women in uniforms with shiny medals came marching down the avenue. Right up in the very front was Marco's grandfather.

"Abuelo!" Marco shouted and waved his hands.
"Why is your grandfather in the parade?" Jenna asked.
Marco stood tall. "My grandfather is a hero."

Abuelo put out his arms and Marco ran and climbed into his lap.

"Happy Memorial Day, Marco," Abuelo said.

Marco threw his arms around Abuelo's neck. "Happy memory day, Abuelo."

He took the butterscotch out of his pocket and pressed it into his grandfather's warm hand.

Marco did not need to ask Mama. He knew this was the best memory day surprise of all.